I Can't Open It!

Push

Paul Shipton
Illustrated by Claire Chrystall

Rigby

Chelsea and Harry went to the bookstore.

BOOKSTORE

Pull

Book
Sale
Book
Sale

3

Harry pushed and pushed.
"I can't open this door,"
he said.

"Don't push," said Chelsea.
"Pull."
Harry pulled.
The door opened.

Pull

7

Then Chelsea and Harry
went to the toy store.

9

Harry pulled and pulled.
"I can't open this door,"
he said.

"Don't pull," said Chelsea.
"Push."
Harry pushed.
The door opened.

13

Then Chelsea and Harry went to the supermarket.

Harry didn't push.
He didn't pull, but
the door opened!